Chapatti Moon

Pippa Goodhart • Lizzie Finlay

With love and thanks to my very good writing group friends, Debbie, Josephine, Alex, Ros and Bridget, each of whom have helped this book to develop over the years – P. G.

For Lambert and Jo – L. F.

TAMARIND

UK | USA | Canada | Ireland | Australia
India | New Zealand | South Africa

Tamarind is part of the Penguin Random House
group of companies whose addresses can be found at
global.penguinrandomhouse.com.

www.penguin.co.uk   www.puffin.co.uk   www.ladybird.co.uk

Penguin
Random House
UK

First published 2017
001

Text copyright © Pippa Goodhart, 2017
Illustrations copyright © Lizzie Finlay, 2017
The moral right of the author and illustrator has been asserted

Printed in China
A CIP catalogue record for this book is available from the British Library

ISBN: 978–1–848–53128–4

All correspondence to:
Tamarind, Penguin Random House Children's,
80 Strand, London WC2R 0RL

Mrs Kapoor
was hungry.

So she decided to
cook up a feast.

She chopped chillies
and garlic and onion
and tomatoes.

She pounded spices
and she tore
coriander.

She cut up aubergines and cauliflower, potatoes and carrots.

She podded peas and wilted spinach.

She scooped yoghurt, and poured coconut milk.

She sizzled
and stirred

and
simmered

Mrs Kapoor
heated pans,
and melted ghee.

to make dosas, masalas,
pakoras, samosas
and chutneys,

all steaming

and creaming

and
sprinkled

and bubbling

and smelling . . .

"Mmm, wonderful!"
said Mrs Kapoor.

She put the food into pots and on
to plates, with spoons and pickle
prongs and a pile of napkins,
all on to her hostess trolley.

Then Mrs Kapoor
made chapattis.

She mixed flour and
water, and shaped
the dough into a ball.

She rolled a chapatti, flat and round,

then put it into a big hot pan,
where it began to puff and crisp
and turn wonderfully golden.
"Perfect," said Mrs Kapoor.

But as she took the chapatti
out of the pan . . .

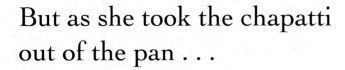

Mrs Kapoor jumped with surprise,
tossing the chapatti
on to the floor,
where it rolled over
and over,
and
out of
the door!

She chased the chapatti,
and so did some more.

The chapatti went rolling off down the road.

"I'm going to catch it!" said Mrs Kapoor.

She tried to snatch it,

but . . .

. . . a boy, thinking it was a ball,
kicked the chapatti over a wall, where . . .

. . . a quick girl
caught it,

and threw it to a man

who said, "That's
not a frisbee!"

Then both of them ran after
the chapatti which came down to land . . .

... in the market place,
where it went

Mosaic

chop chop
BUTCHER

Julie's

COFFEE

bouncing and tripping

and jumping and slipping

Mrs Kapoor was
about to catch it
when a goat gave a butt
that biffed it down the hill.

It was racing away again until . . .

"I'll ride my trolley!"
said Mrs Kapoor,
and off she went
over lumps
and bumps –

Lumpety-
bumpety,
rattle and roll.

She was catching up with the chapatti at last,
when a donkey *hee-hawed* and gave

a great

big

KICK!

HEE-HAW!

Up rose the chapatti
into the sky . . . .

where it glowed
like a luminous
lantern, or . . . .

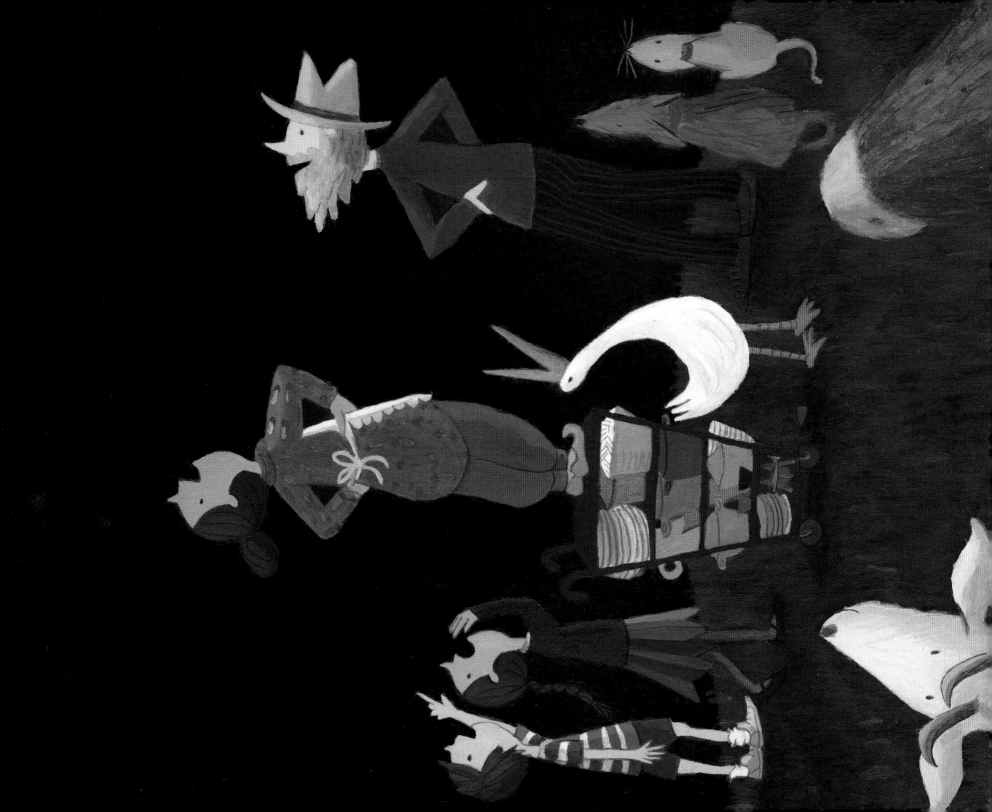

"A chapatti moon!" said Mrs Kapoor.
"Let's all share a moonlit picnic!"

So, in the creamy cool light
of the chapatti moon,

they danced and laughed and ate, and soon . . .

they slumped into slumber.
All except for our very good friend Mrs Kapoor who
was still awake and still hungry – until she saw . . .

. . . her chapatti moon slip-sliding down the sky.
She held out her hands,
and she caught it.

"I shall eat the moon!"
said Mrs Kapoor.

It was just enough.
She wanted no more.

And it did taste
wonderfully moony.

Goodnight, goodnight,
Mrs Kapoor.